RICHIE IN MY RECITAL

ME IN THE NUTCRACKER...

ME MAKING A SLAP SHOT

ME BEING BODY CHECKED DURING THE HOCKEY GAME

RICHIE MAKING A SLAP SHOT...

RICHIE HAVING A SLIGHT DIFFERENCE OF OPINION WITH ANOTHER PLAYER....

OSCEOLA LIBRARY SYSTEM FLORIDA

P9-CQV-608

Dedicated to my rotten redheaded brother,
Richard Barber.

OUR MOM LOVED US BOTH more than anything. She always told us that. She saw to it that Richie could play hockey on the junior team and I could take ballet at Miss Barrent's Ballet School. Richie had his precious old hockey team, but ballet was my life!

Even Miss Barrent said I showed great promise.

What I loved about ballet class was . . . Richie wasn't there!

Rotten Richie and the Ultimate Dare

Patricia Polacco

PHILOMEL BOOKS

As if life wasn't bad enough having to endure my rotten redheaded older brother all summer, my mom, brother and I had to move away from Grampa and Gramma's farm in Union City to Battle Creek to be closer to Mom's teaching job. Now I was going to be the new kid at school. But even worse than that, my rotten brother was going to be in the same school as I was. He was the black hole in my universe. The embarrassment of my life. The

frog in my punch bowl. The spider in my cereal. The wart on my cookie. The slug in my Jell-O. The snake in my soup. In other words, this new school was going to be a disaster. All because of him!

I mean, he picked his nose and looked at it. He chewed with his mouth open. He spat when he talked. He made rude noises with his armpits. And odor! My rotten redheaded older brother stank! He reeked of stale bubble gum mixed with rancid peanut butter and putrid gym socks with overtones of wet puppy.

At school he was everywhere. Our first day at Fremont Elementary School, Richie put fake dog poop in the middle of the hall floor. He even poured water onto it so it looked real. Then he stood and watched as the whole school was plastered against the walls trying to walk around it. He'd struck again. Then, just as I passed, he hollered, "Hey, look . . . there's my little sister!"

I wanted to die!

As time passed, I managed to make some good friends. After all, they knew it wasn't my fault to have someone like Richie in my family.

One night at the dinner table, I was telling Mom about ballet class and our upcoming recital.

"I heard the mayor will be there, his daughter dances at Miss Barrent's . . . and Momma, Miss Barrent picked me to do the special adagio with Paul LeBlanc," I squealed. "He's the best dancer in the whole school!"

My brother snorted and rolled his eyes.

"Look, Momma, I do a *grand tour jeté* and a *rond de jambe en l'air* . . . and almost thirty-six *relevés*." I got up and demonstrated.

Mom clapped and cheered.

"Aw, I can do that with my eyes closed," Richie croaked.

"You can not!" I protested.

"Can too!" he countered.

"Can not!" I screamed.

"Too," he said with a sneer.

"Well, ballet is harder than dumb old hockey any day!" I hollered.

"Is not," he chortled.

"All hockey is . . . is . . . skating around in circles with a crooked stick

chasing a little lump of rubber. Babies can do that!" I bellowed.

"Stop it, both of you," Mom scolded. "What difference does it make as long as you both are doing what you enjoy?"

All the rest of the evening, Richie danced around me on his tippy-toes, making rude sounds.

"Tweet, tweet," he teased.

And just before I got into bed, he stuck his head in my doorway and made kissing sounds and said, "Trisha's in love with Paul LeBlanc . . . tweet, tweet, tweet."

The next morning at school, I could hear his weaselly voice echo down the hallways. He was telling his greasy little friends on the hockey team about my doing a ballet duet with Paul LeBlanc. Then they all laughed and made tweeting sounds and danced around on their tiptoes too.

They kept it up all day.

Finally, I had enough. At recess my two friends from ballet class and I marched up to Richie and his friends on the hockey team.

"Oh, Richie," I cooed. "If you think ballet is so darn easy, come to my ballet school. Be in my recital." I crossed my arms and waited for his answer.

Richie's friends chuckled, but they were watching Richie to see what he would do.

"Humph" is all he could manage to say.

"I dare you," I said defiantly as a crowd gathered around us.

Richie's eyes darted around nervously.

Now I had him! "I double dare you," I added as I drew up nose to nose.

His friends snapped to attention. They all eyed Richie.

Richie just stood there snorting and steaming at me.

"I triple dog dare you . . . with skin-do's and two-ups!" I sneered.

His friends reeled in disbelief. I had breached etiquette in passing double dog dare and going directly to the triple with skin-do's and two-ups.

Now there was no way out for him. He had to accept.

He kicked the ground. "Wellllllll," he muttered. Then his eyes narrowed. "Okay, okay . . . I'll do it." I looked triumphant as everyone cheered.

Richie and his teammates suddenly dropped to a close huddle. They whispered for a time, then they all looked at me.

"On one condition." Richie leered. "I'll go to your dumb ol' ballet classes, learn your dumb ol' dances and be in your stupid ol' recital . . . but only if you practice with the team and play one game with us."

His teammates glared at me.

I thought for a moment. After all, I had poise, great balance, endless stamina. Ballet had given me all that. And hockey was only *skating*, and I

loved to skate. What could be so hard about this?!

"Okay, dog breath, you're on!" I heard myself saying.

"Okay, twerp, our game is next week. So you'll have a week to practice."

"No sweat, burlap!" I shot back. "You'll have a month to practice for my recital."

Richie got permission from his coach and the league to let me practice and play just one game. I guess it wasn't easy, but he managed to do it.

I practiced hard—all week.

The next week, all of Fremont Elementary School was there for the game. Even Mr. Thomas, the principal. He and all of the teachers were in the front row. I was a little nervous.

The coach's wife helped me suit up in the closet of the locker room.

"Geez, this stuff is heavier than it looks," I said to her.

"Well, dear, this is a contact sport and we have to protect your bones from breaking and your teeth from getting knocked out!" she said cheerfully.

Bones? Teeth? I began to wonder if I had bitten off more than I could chew.

That was assuming I'd even be able to do that after this game.

By the time Richie helped me out onto the ice with the rest of the team, I could hardly stand up. But the more I skated around, the better I felt.

A whistle blew and everyone cheered for our team. THE BATTLE CREEK BEAVERS! I raised my hand to wave and fell flat on my behind. It was slippery out there! One of the Beavers helped me up.

That's when I saw the team we were playing against explode onto the ice. My stomach turned. THE SAGINAW SONICS! Each and every one of them must have weighed 400 pounds.

PENALTY BOX

BEAVERS

"Face-off!" the referee called out as the two captains faced off.

They looked real mean at each other. The referee was about to drop the puck between them.

"Where do I go, Richie?" I called out to my brother down the line.

"Just stay out of our way! When that puck hits the ice, the race is on."

Then the ref dropped it. There was a blur of sticks, flashing jerseys and pinging skate blades. I headed straight for the wall to hang on. I saw the puck heading for me. It bounced off the wall and stopped right next to me.

I just stood and looked at it. "Hit it, hit it!" the Beavers yelled at me.

I heard what sounded like a locomotive and saw the Saginaw Sonics closing in. Boom! They plastered me against the wall. Their sticks zinged, banged and cracked as they tried to get the puck.

Finally a whistle blew and they piled off of me. All that padding sure didn't seem to help much.

"You let 'em bodycheck you, twerp. I told you to stay out of the way!" my brother yelled as he zoomed by.

The teams faced off over and over again. Now I knew what to do. Stay away from both teams.

I saw Richie line up the perfect shot at the Sonics' goal. Just as he was about to slap it in, one of the Sonics put out his stick and tripped him.

I steamed right up to that big old Sonic and beaned him with my stick.

"You're not playing fair!" I screamed.

I heard a whistle blow. The referee grabbed me, opened the side gate and threw me onto a bench.

"High-sticking," he bellowed. "Penalty goes against the Beavers, Number Twelve, five minutes in the penalty box!"

So that's what was happening. This was sweet. All I had to do was trip a Sonic with my stick and I would be sent to the penalty box.

I could stay in here for the whole game!

By golly, my plan worked like a charm. I spent almost the entire game in the penalty box. By the third period the score was four to four. Our team had played a great game. The Beavers outskated, outshot and outplayed the Sonics on every front. And just as we were going to score the winning goal, all of the Sonics piled onto all the Beavers and started a fight.

When the fight was over, almost all of the Sonics, except the goalie, were in the penalty box. All of the Beavers were too. "You're back out on the ice, Twelve. Let's go," the ref barked as he opened the door and pushed me out.

There I was, all by myself, out on that ice with the biggest, meanest, ugliest Sonic of all!

It was their shot and I, alone, had to guard our goal. I hung on to the net for dear life. The crowd was dead silent. The puck was dropped and that Sonic barreled down the ice, heading straight for me.

I heard him make a slap shot. Then I saw him leap into the air and land right on top of the net. He bounced off. Then he just lay there, out cold.

That's when I felt it. I had the puck in my hand. He hadn't made the goal. I'd caught it! The crowd exploded.

"Skate the puck to their goal, twerp. You have thirty seconds to do it!" I heard my brother yell.

I steadied the puck with my stick and pushed it ahead of me as fast as I could. The Sonics' goal seemed miles away. The clock was ticking; the crowd was calling out the seconds. Then the puck got away from me. I slid back up to it, closed my eyes and slapped that puck as hard as I could.

The buzzer sounded the end of the game. It was all over. When I opened my eyes, there it was, the puck smack in the Sonics' net. I had scored the winning point!

"That's my little sister!" I heard my brother call out as the crowd roared.

Well, I guess I showed Richie all right. I had to admit, though, hockey was not the piece of cake I'd thought.

But now it was Richie's turn. He had to come to my ballet classes and dance in my recital.

Richie was good to his word. He practiced hard and even stopped teasing me about Paul LeBlanc.

Finally, the night of the recital arrived. All of Miss Barrent's Ballet School students were in a dither.

Richie and I were in the dressing room. "I ain't wearing this," he hissed as I held up his costume. "I'll look like a flower, and all my friends will be out there tonight."

"I had to wear your hockey gear, so you *are* wearing it!" I insisted.

Richie complained as we all did our warm-up at the *barre*. He complained when we put on our stage makeup, and he complained that after all that he was too exhausted to go on.

"Guess it's not as easy as you thought, huh," I sneered.

We peeked out of the curtain. The whole school was there. Again.

Richie turned so red, his freckles almost disappeared!

"Onstage . . . onstage, people," Miss Barrent called out as she clapped her hands. We took our places onstage. The music began and the curtains parted. All of us were in a perfect fifth positions.

All except Richie.

His feet were turned in instead of out as we started our dance in unison.

He jumped when we glided. He twirled when we leaped. When we *glissaded* upstage, he *glissaded* downstage. When we did our *pas de chat*, Richie hopped around like a rabbit.

And at the end of the number, as we all did our *grand arabesque*, Richie lost his balance and grabbed for the curtain.

That's when the audience started to snicker.

The next two numbers went very well—because Richie wasn't in them!

Richie hid from all of us during the intermission.

Then it was time for the Nyeela number, the main number of the second part of the recital.

Richie was a wood nymph. All he had to do was one single *tour jeté* . . . Just one *tour jeté*.

Well, he did it, all right, and landed right on Paul LeBlanc. Paul lost his balance and fell into a fairy tree. The tree tipped, knocked over a gazebo and finally fell through the backdrop!

As we were all doing our twirls across the floor, we knew to watch a spot so that we wouldn't get dizzy. Richie didn't. So he twirled and got so dizzy that this time he grabbed the curtain and almost swung off the stage.

The audience roared with laughter.

The curtain closed for the second intermission. Miss Barrent held her head. "Your brother has ruined the entire production!" she shrieked.

Then she collapsed in a heap in a director's chair and glared at me.

"Miss Barrent, we still have the finale. The adagio duet with Paul and me. We have our closing solos," I pleaded.

Miss Barrent managed a weak smile, only to be replaced with utter horror as Paul LeBlanc limped toward her.

"Miss Barrent, I can't do the last number!" he wailed. "I sprained my ankle when Richie fell on me."

I wanted to cry. We all looked at Richie and just shook our heads. Richie saw the tears well up in my eyes. "Wait!" he called out. "I can do Paul's number."

Everyone groaned.

"You have done enough tonight, Richard," Miss Barrent said sadly.

"No, Miss Barrent, I really can! I've been practicing all of the steps to help Trisha rehearse. I can do it with my eyes closed."

"Miss Barrent, maybe he really can," I said. "He has been practicing those steps. The grand lift at the end is the only one that still needs work."

"Please let me try," Richie pleaded.

Miss Barrent finally agreed, but "no lift at the end."

Paul's costume fit Richie perfectly.

We took center stage. The music started and the curtain opened.

The audience started to giggle. But as we took our first steps, Richie was in complete unison with me. He lifted me when he was supposed to. He was doing the right steps in time with the music. He was actually graceful. The audience wasn't laughing anymore.

Then Richie took his pose while I did my solo. I danced around the entire stage and then did thirty-six consecutive *relevés* across the stage *en pointe*.

Everyone leapt to their feet and cheered.

Then I posed and it was Richie's turn to take Paul's solo.

I had no idea what he was going to do. I wasn't sure if he knew all of Paul's dance. To my astonishment Richie did the highest leaps I had ever seen. The audience clapped. And then he was ready for the final *pirouette*. He pointed, snapped his leg in a *jeté* and spun. He was a blur! He must have done ten consecutive turns.

I lost count!

Richie gestured for me to join him. Paul and I were supposed to do the grand leap here.

"Richie, we can't do this," I whispered.

"Come on, kid. Let's give them their money's worth." He winked.

He whirled me around and lifted me above his head. He threw me up and caught me, then spun me out. I ran stage left and did *grand jetés*.

As the music built, it was my cue to run and leap into Richie's arms. He was to lift me over his head and hold me there while he spun and hurled me into my last *arabesque*. My heart was in my throat.

I looked at his face. I closed my eyes and ran directly at him. I leapt high into the air.

"Please don't let Richie mess up!" I prayed. I was airborne. I could see Miss Barrent cover her mouth and gasp. I was airborne.

Richie caught me!

It was perfect. Perfect. WE NAILED IT! The audience jumped to their feet and roared, cheered and clapped.

"That's my brother," I heard myself saying.

That night, as we all sat in front of the fire at home, Richie finally said to me, "Okay, okay, ballet is harder than I thought. I really had to practice to do it right."

"Well," I added, "I'd have to say that hockey is way cool, and it takes a lot just to play the game . . ."

"Truce, then, Slapshot," Richie said, holding out his little finger.

"Okay, Dance King . . . truce," I said as we locked our fingers.

RICHARD EVEN ADMITTED TO ME years later that his short course on ballet helped him on the ice. And the balance that it took for me just to stand on skates helped me in dancing, that's for sure.

To this day, he still calls me Slapshot, and I still call him Dance King.

Patricia Lee Gauch, Editor

PHILOMEL BOOKS
A division of Penguin Young Readers Group.
Published by The Penguin Group.
Penguin Group (USA) Inc., 375 Hudson Street, New York, NY 10014, U.S.A.
Penguin Group (Canada), 90 Eglinton Avenue East, Suite 700, Toronto, Ontario, Canada M4P 2Y3
(a division of Pearson Penguin Canada Inc.).
Penguin Books Ltd, 80 Strand, London WC2R 0RL, England.
Penguin Ireland, 25 St. Stephen's Green, Dublin 2, Ireland (a division of Penguin Books Ltd.).
Penguin Group (Australia), 250 Camberwell Road, Camberwell, Victoria 3124, Australia
(a division of Pearson Australia Group Pty Ltd).
Penguin Books India Pvt Ltd, 11 Community Centre, Panchsheel Park, New Delhi - 110 017, India.
Penguin Group (NZ), Cnr Airborne and Rosedale Roads, Albany, Auckland 1310, New Zealand
(a division of Pearson New Zealand Ltd).
Penguin Books (South Africa) (Pty) Ltd, 24 Sturdee Avenue, Rosebank, Johannesburg 2196, South Africa.
Penguin Books Ltd, Registered Offices: 80 Strand, London WC2R 0RL, England.

All rights reserved. This book, or parts thereof, may not be reproduced in any form without permission in writing
from the publisher, Philomel Books, a division of Penguin Young Readers Group, 345 Hudson Street, New
York, NY 10014. Philomel Books, Reg. U.S. Pat. & Tm. Off. The scanning, uploading and distribution of this
book via the Internet or via any other means without the permission of the publisher is illegal and punishable
by law. Please purchase only authorized electronic editions, and do not participate in or encourage electronic
piracy of copyrighted materials. Your support of the author's rights is appreciated. The publisher does not have
any control over and does not assume any responsibility for author or third-party websites or their content.
Published simultaneously in Canada.   Manufactured in China by South China Printing Co. Ltd.
Design by Semadar Megged.
The illustrations are rendered in pencils and markers.
Library of Congress Cataloging-in-Publication Data
Polacco, Patricia.   Rotten Richie and the ultimate dare / Patricia Polacco.   p. cm.
Summary: Richie and his younger sister Trisha face off in a contest to see whose hobby is more challenging.
[1. Contests—Fiction. 2. Hobbies—Fiction. 3. Brothers and sisters—Fiction.] I. Title.
PZ7.P75186Rot 2006   [E]—dc22   2005025050
ISBN 0-399-24531-6
1 3 5 7 9 10 8 6 4 2
First Impression

RICHIE....

ME DANCING

RICHIE, ME WITH HIS SON, BEN - A HOCKEY PLAYER

SECOND TIME ON TOE....

ME AS A WOOD NYMPH...

RICHIE FALLS DURING BALLET CLASS....